I0669757

Harry Bache Smith, Reginald De Koven

Robin Hood

a comic opera in three acts

Harry Bache Smith, Reginald De Koven

Robin Hood
a comic opera in three acts

ISBN/EAN: 9783337368296

Printed in Europe, USA, Canada, Australia, Japan

Cover: Foto ©Andreas Hilbeck / pixelio.de

More available books at **www.hansebooks.com**

ROBIN HOOD,

A

COMIC OPERA

IN

THREE ACTS.

———

MUSIC BY

REGINALD DeKOVEN,

LIBRETTO BY

HARRY B. SMITH.

———

COPYRIGHT, 1890, BY HARRY B. SMITH.

———

NEW YORK:
BURR PRINTING HOUSE,
18 JACOB STREET,
1896.

CHARACTERS REPRESENTED.

ROBERT.....................Earl of Huntington, afterward Robin Hood.

SIR TRISTRAM TESTY..........................Sheriff of Nottingham.

LITTLE JOHN,
FRIAR TUCK,
ALLAN-A-DALE, } ....Outlaws.
WILL SCARLET,
GUY OF GISBORNE.

MARIAN.....Daughter of Lord Fitzwalter, afterward called Maid Marian.

DAME DURDEN.......Keeper of an Inn on the Border of Sherwood Forest.

ANNABEL.. Her Daughter.

MARK O' THE MILL..................................... A Villager.

Outlaws, King's Foresters, Villagers, Sheriff's Henchmen, Village
Musicians, Milkmaids, Shepherds, etc., etc.

ROBIN HOOD.

ACT I.

SCENE. *The old town of Nottingham. Early morning on the day of the May Day fair. Villagers enter preparing for the fair.*

Villagers.

'Tis the morning of the fair,
'Tis a day of pastime rare ;
Hail the gladsome day,
The happy time of May.
Springtime cometh over hill and vale.
May Day bright
Brings delight.
Happy time, we sing to thee all hail.
Birds so bright carol on ev'ry side ;
Seem to sing
To the spring,
Welcoming with joy the sweet springtide.

(A pedlar enters with his pack. Outlaws' horns are heard in the distance.)

All.

List to the gay hunter's horn
Sound through the forest at morn.

(Little John, Allan-a-Dale and Will Scarlet enter.)

Little John.

In Sherwood forest, the merriest of lives
Is our life so fair and free.

Scarlet.

We roam and rove
In Sherwood's grove
Beneath the greenwood tree.

Allan.

Through all the glades
And sylvan shades
Our homes are found.
We hunt the deer.
Afar and near
Our hunting horns resound.
Tan-ta ra !

4

The three.	Cheerily, merrily, roaming e'er,
	Living like kings in the forest fair ;
	Never are we weary, ever we are gay.
	Free are we as birds the livelong summer day.
All.	Cheerily, merrily, etc.

(Annabel enters from cottage R.)

Annabel.	Surely 'tis an acquisition
	To this goodly companie ;
	Outlaws of such high position
	Gladly at the fair we see.
All.	Come and join our dance !

MORRIS DANCE.

All.	Fal-la, Fal-la
	Trip a morris dance hilarious.
	Lightly, brightly,
	Trip in measures multifarious.
	Dance so happily, so gaily, madly,
	Dance your prettiest, your lightest and best ;
	No court minuet is danced half so gladly,
	Dance your liveliest and don't stop to rest.
	Fal-la, Fal-la.

Friar Tuck. (*Outside singing.*) Who so gay as the jolly friar !

Little John. Here comes our jolly comrade, Friar Tuck.

All. Hurrah !

(Enter Friar Tuck.)

Little John. How comes it that you are here at our fair, when you should be at home counting your beads and mumbling your orisons ?

Friar Tuck. Good, my son and merry master. I've had a right busy day. I've been selling goods.

All. Goods ?

Friar Tuck. Yes! Our goods—goods we've confiscated—absorbed ; clothing, deer, and so forth. And our arch enemy, the high sheriff, was there, disguised as a mountebank. He bought goods of me—an old suit of homespun, ragged and torn, three crowns (*all laugh*), and an old starved deer for eight crowns. (*All laugh.*)

Scarlet. A King's deer, I'll be sworn !

Friar Tuck. Better yet, from his own park.

Scarlet. Did he pay for them ?

Friar Tuck. No ! No !

(Little John snatches purse from Tuck.)

Little John. Well, as leader of the band, I propose that we go to the nearest hostelry and spend the proceeds.

Friar Tuck. Agreed ! And if the tipple is good you'll find that I have a throat on me like a pelican.

(Exit Little John, Scarlet, Allan-a-Dale, and Friar Tuck, L. U. E.)

MILKMAIDS' CHORUS.

Milkmaids.
When chanticleer crowing
Says night is a'going,
And larks their nests are scorning–O,
In rain or fair weather,
We trip o'er the heather
So early in the morning–O.
Yes, when dawn's first blush we see
Come we milkmaids o'er the lea,
Singing tra-la-la.
Plowboys haste o'er dell and hill,
Whistling with a right good-will,
Piping their tra-la-la.

(Annabel comes forward.)

Annabel.
With a lissome figure and a laughing face
An ideal milkmaid's a thing of grace.
A creature whose laughing, dimpled face
Is of lilies and roses the trysting place.
The painters depict her a fairy thing ;
The poets her praises delight to sing.
She dresses in satins and finest silks,
She sings sweet songs as she sits and milks.
She insists upon wearing a Gainsborough hat,
Her ankles are something to wonder at.
Her hands are dainty and oh, so white ;
Her curls are perfect, her eyes are bright.
She's the manner and mien of my lady fine.
While even her cows are idyllic kine.
Such milkmaids do poets and painters find,
And it's proper to add we are just that kind.

Milkmaids.
We're exceedingly glad
We have nothing to add
In the way of contradiction,
For it's easy to see
That such milkmaids as we
Are not milkmaids of fact, but of fiction.

Allan.
But the kind of milkmaids that you describe
Do not belong to the real tribe

The real milkmaid in a homespun gown
Has very few smiles but full many a frown ;
Her hands are heavy and red and rough,
And she rarely sings, for her voice is gruff.
She is middle-aged, she is plain at that,
And her figure is something to cavil at.
Her life is a merry round, 'tis said,
Of rising, working and going to bed.
Her joy is getting her work all done
And going to rest at the set of sun.
Of all her life, 'tis the saddest tale
When a cow kicks over a brimming pail.
Her hands are rough, and her gown homespun,
And she only sings when her work is done.

Milkmaids.　　　　　We're exceedingly sure
　　　　　　　　　We could never endure
　　　　　　　　Any life so fraught with friction ;
　　　　　　　　　And 'tis easy to see
　　　　　　　　　That it's nicer to be
　　　　　　　　A milkmaid of fanciful fiction.

Dame D. (*To Annabel.*) Thou pert minx ! Get thee within. (*To Allan.*)
Young man, begone, unless thou hast a mind to buy butter or cheese
from a lone widow and her daughter.

Allan. Butter and cheese? peaches and cream ! (*Allan kisses Annabel.*)

Dame D. Eh ? What was that ?

Allan. 'Twas nothing, gentle Dame.

Dame D. Truly a loud nothing. This smacks of untruth.

Allan (*sympathetically*). Is it true that you are a widow ?

Dame D. (*Aside.*) Can he mean to propose (*Sighs.*) Alas ! I know not
for surety. My man has been at the Crusades for twelve years. Each
year I have sent him a suit of homespun and a letter, but to the
last I have received no answer. I fear the outlaws waylaid the messenger and stole the suit.

Allan. Perhaps your good man may return this very day. Many bowmen
from the Crusades will attend the fair to take part in the shooting
match, and it is time for the archers to be here.

　　　　　　　　　(*Horn sounds without.*)

Allan. Yes, there is the signal for their coming.

Dame D. (*Looking off.*) But who is the gallant leading them ? Surely he
is not a forester.

Allan. That is young Robert of Huntington. He comes into his title and
estates this very day.

Annabel. (*Looking off.*) Methinks he is a proper man.

Allan. He is a fine fellow, and though he belongs to the nobility he is the finest bow-shot in all England. Oh, what a pity that he is not an outlaw.

(*Horns heard. The archers enter headed by Robert, Little John, Allan-a-Dale, Scarlet—All armed with long bows.*)

ENSEMBLE.

Archers.	Come the bowmen in Lincoln green,
	More skillful archers were never seen.
Villagers.	Bowmen they with eyes so keen,
	Gaily clad in Lincoln green.
Robert.	In the leafy shades
	Of the woodland glades,

'Neath old Sherwood's greenwood tree ;
Where the red deer springs
And the throstle sings
Is the dearest spot to me ;
For never a care
I' the world comes there,
And never you hear a sigh ;
As you love and laugh,
As you quip and quaff,
So gaily the days go by.
Then hey for the merry greenwood ? say I,
And give me a bow of yew ;
Let mine be the life that is free from strife,
Where friends are stanch and true.

All.	Then hey for the merry greenwood ! say I, etc.
Robert.	Oh, we hunt the stag
	Over hill and crag.

Where the antlered monarch bounds ;
With a trusty bow
We can lay him low,
Then our ringing bugle sounds.
All lovers who mourn
Can find hope newborn
If the life of the woods they try ;
There is sure relief
For a lover's grief,
So gaily the days go by.

All.	Then hey for the merry greenwood ! say I, etc.
Annabel.	Sir cavalier,
	You're welcome here
	To this our fair.

Robert.	My thanks, my dear,
	A pretty girl
	You are, I swear.
Allan.	Just pardon me,
	My friend, but she
	Is my betrothed I must aver.
Little J. (Aside to Robert.)	Though all is fair
	In love and war,
	You'd better not make love to her.
Robert.	As all is fair
	In love or war,
	I'll make love to whome'er I will;
	On May Day bright,
	When hearts are light,
	I scoff at him who takes it ill.

MADRIGAL.

Annabel, Allan, Robert, and Little John.

All is fair in love and war,
    So they say, so they say.
    (*With a heigho and a lily gay.*)
And a wight can rightly win
    Any maid on May Day.
    (*As the primrose spreads so sweetly.*)
Lily bells begin to ring,
    Fal la-la!
'Tis the matin time of spring,
    Fal-la la!
Maiden fancies love to stray,
    So they say, so they say.
    (*With a heigho and a lily gay.*)
Birds all choose their mates in May,
    So they say, so they say.
    (*As the primrose spreads so sweetly.*)
When the ringdoves are a'cooing,
And the redbreasts are a'wooing,
Then methinks, if ne'er before,
All is fair in love and war.
    Fal-la-la, la-la, etc.

(*Commotion without. Marian, dressed as a cavalier, enters, pursued by Friar Tuck.*)

Little J.	How now? What's the row?
Allan.	Who is this youthful gallant, pray,
	With whom you seem to seek a fray?

All.	Yes, explain.
Marian.	Yes, please explain to me for one,
	I'd like to know what I have done.
	He wants to fight, this priestly churl,
	Because I kissed a pretty girl.
All.	What girl? Explain.
Friar T.	When I can get my breath I'll tell,
	Just what befell.
	I saw this little coxcomb here
	Make love unto a pretty dear,
	And give her a resounding kiss
	Upon the cheek—about like this. (*Tries to kiss Annabel.*)
All.	Down with him!
Robert.	Nay! Hold! It seems to me extremely flat
	To fight about a little thing like that.
Marian.	I never offered such a kiss.
	'Twas just a tiny one like this. (*Offers a kiss to Annabel.*)
Allan.	You seem to think it is a feat
	To kiss each pretty girl you meet.

SOLO. *Marian.*

I come as a cavalier,
   And you must take it not amiss ;
I do as a cavalier,
   Who is never loath to steal a kiss.
And never a cavalier,
   Would be a gallant knight and true,
Who wouldn't confer a kiss
   Upon a girl who wished him to.
Cavaliers, I declare.
Must be courteous to the fair.
Cavaliers e'er must be
In their manners slightly free.
And if you had been by,
You would have done just as I.
Wrath pray stifle,
'Twas a trifle,
She herself could not deny.

All.	Cavaliers, we declare, etc.

(*All march off excepting Robert and Marian.*)

Marian. (*Aside.*) So this is the future Earl of Huntington whom the King has commanded me to marry. Well, he's not so bad after all. (*Addressing Robert.*) Young fellow, can you tell one where one may find Robert who is to be Earl of Huntington?

Robert. Yes, young fellow ; I can tell one, or, for that matter, I might tell two, for I am he.

Marian. Well, I suppose you know that you are commanded to be married ?

Robert. Commanded to be married ?

Marian. Yes ; behold the King's command. (*Produces parchment.*)

Robert. And what have you to do with it ?

Marian. Oh, I am the page who brings the King's message to Lady Marian's guardian, the Sheriff of Nottingham.

Robert. Look ye, young sir, Robert, Earl of Huntington, is not the man to marry the first girl that is offered to him. *I* am rather particular.

Marian. Oh, indeed. Well, you may as well understand that my cousin Marian is not the girl to marry off-hand. She's not easy to please, and I don't think you will suit.

Robert. Oh, indeed ; and has she a high-born temper like her cousin's ?

Marian. If you want to know what she looks like, you might take a glance at me. We are said to favor each other.

Robert. Not a bad-looking young fellow. So you favor each other, do you ? Well, suppose you favor *me* by telling your cousin that I am not ready to marry, and therefore I respectfully refuse her.

Marian. What ! Such impudence ! You refuse my cousin who has had dozens of offers from the finest gallants in England ? You refuse her indeed ? *She* refuses *you.*

Robert. (*Aside.*) That was a regular feminine outburst. Why, this must be Lady Marian herself. Rather pretty—and clever, too. (*To Marian.*) Really, my dear boy, I was only teasing you. The fact is that I love your cousin, and I am delighted at the King's command. Oh, she is adorable.

Marian. Why, where have you seen me ? (*Recollects herself suddenly.*)

Robert. Aha ! Caught by your own confession. And did you suppose that I did not recognize you from the first ?

Marian. It was only natural that I should want to see the kind of man that I am commanded to marry. I took the place of the page who was to bring the order to the Sheriff, Sir Tristram Testy. He is the custodian of my fortune.

Robert. Sir Tristram has charge of my estates as well. This Sir Tristram seems very fond of being custodian of estates. I mistrust him.

Marian. And I suspect him, too. He has been pressing the suit of one Guy of Gisborne, whom he wishes me to marry. The two have some conspiracy afoot. Sir Tristram is likely to be here soon to attend the fair. I will dress as a village girl, take a place in yonder dairy booth, and try to learn his motive in wishing me to marry Guy of Gisborne.

Robert. Marry another ! How can you speak of such a thing? Are you not plighted to me by the King's command ?

Marian. But you refused me.

Robert. Refuse ? No ; never did King have subject who obeyed more willingly. (*About to put his arm around her*)

Marian. (*Repulsing him.*) Not so fast. (*Imitating his manner in the early part of the scene.*) Look ye, young sir, Lady Marian Fitzwalter is not the girl to marry the first man who is offered to her. I am rather particular.

Robert. Believe me ; I spoke the truth when I told you that at the court tourneys I have seen you and seen only to dream of your beauty for days. But I never thought that I should have the happiness of calling you mine.

DUET. *Marian and Robert.*

Robert.	Though it was within this hour we met,
	I have dreamed of such a face as thine,
	Dreams I love to think of even yet
	When I held thy little hand in mine—
	To wake was for that dreamland face to pine.
Marian.	Dreams we must by contraries divine.
Robert.	Will that dream come true ?
Marian.	No, no.
Robert.	Let me dream anew.
Marian.	Not so.
	Who knows what fate
	May thee await,
	If thy constancy time and distance prove.
	This hand of mine
	May yet be thine
	If fidelity dwelleth with thy love.
Robert.	Long, long ago,
	Some time, I know,
	In dreamland fair we met.
Marian.	It may be so, but I forget.
	I needs must own
	That thou alone
	Art to me more than all beside.
Robert.	What joy to hear
	Those words so dear.
Both.	Love ever will be our guide.
	Come dream so bright,
	My heart delight.
	Dreaming anew.
	I find 'tis true.
	Fair dost thou seem,
	Beautiful dream.
	At last I see thee,
	My dream has come true.

(They exit. The Sheriff and Sir Guy enter attended by guards, foresters and villagers.)

SONG. *The Sheriff.*

I am the Sheriff of Nottingham,
 My eye is like an eagle's ;
So sly and clever—in fact I am
 One of the law's best beagles.
 I'm a genius quite.

Guy.   He's a wonderful wight.
Sheriff.   I'm considered remarkably bright.
 If anyone fractures the slightest law,
 With a glance I can fill him with panic awe.
All.   Bow low !
Guy.   Bow lowly as you can.
All.   Bow low !
Sheriff.   You should to such a man.
    You may search for aye
    But you never will descry
    Such a wondrous Sheriff as I.
    Such a brain——
All.   He makes no error.
Sheriff.   Such an eye——
All.   It striketh terror.

Sheriff. I've a seething brain that can never go astray.
 I am sure to be right alway ;
 Such a Sheriff bold as you behold
 You don't see ev'ry day.

 I never yet made a mistake,
 I'd like to for variety's sake.
 In short, infallible I am,
 The Sheriff of Nottingham.

All.   He never yet made a mistake, etc.
Sheriff.   The merry Sheriff of Nottingham,
    Is always right and lawful :
 If anyone hints he's a sham,
    His punishment is awful.
 I put him in jail.
Guy.   He refuses all bail.
Sheriff.   'Tis an argument ne'er known to fail ;
 If any plebeian my greatness mocks,
 I answer by putting him in the stocks.
All.   Bow low !
Guy.   Bow lowly as you can, etc.

(The chorus exit.)

Sheriff. All is well now, friend Guy. I have evidence enough to send all these outlaws to the gallows. A letter that I found in the pocket of that homespun coat I bought at the auction, proves that it was sent by one Dame Durden to her husband at the Crusades. The messenger must have been robbed by Little John's band. What do you think of that for a piece of detective work ? I fancy it was rather clever of me.

Guy. Oh, I wish I had half your acuteness. I wish you would lend me your eagle eye for a few days.

Sheriff. Patience, good Guy. At present you are a simple country lout.

Guy. Quite right ; so I am.

Sheriff. When you are a peer of England, you can be as loutish as you please.

Guy. A peer of England ! Oh, I would do anything to be a peer of England.

Sheriff. Leave it all to me, and you shall be the Earl of Huntington.

Guy. The Earl of Huntington ! Why, there is one already.

Sheriff. True, there is a person who thinks he is the Earl. He comes of age to-day. He has a fortune of a hundred thousand crowns, which I must deliver to him to-day. Now, if I should make you Earl of Huntington, friend Guy, you would be satisfied with fifty thousand crowns, wouldn t you ?

Guy. Yes ; or twenty-five. Why, I would be Earl of Huntington for my board and lodging.

Sheriff. (Aside.) Well, then, if friend Guy is satisfied with twenty-five, I can worry along on seventy-five. Now, I fancy that was rather clever of me. Now I want you to marry my ward, Lady Marian Fitzwalter——nice girl—rich, too.

Guy. I would even do that to be a peer.

Sheriff. And I suppose you would be satisfied with a dowry of ten thousand crowns ; wouldn't you, friend Guy ?

Guy (doubtfully). How beautiful is she?

Sheriff. Oh, her beauty shames the noon-day sun.

Guy. Why, I would marry a young woman whose beauty shames the noon-day sun for almost nothing.

Sheriff. So it is all arranged. I make you the Earl of Huntington, and you get twenty-five thousand crowns. *(Aside.)* I get seventy-five. *(To Guy.)* You marry Lady Marian and get ten thousand crowns' dowry with her. *(Aside.)* I get ninety thousand. Now I fancy that's very clever of me.

Guy. Oh, how can I ever thank you ?

Sheriff. (Aside.) Now, that's what comes of having an eagle eye.

(Marian enters dressed as a dairy maid. She crosses to the dairy booth unseen by Guy or the Sheriff.)

Guy. But stop a minute. You say I am a simple country lout, and I have no doubt you are right. Now, it's just possible that this lady whose beauty shames the noon-day sun may not fall in love with me at first sight.

Sheriff. Wait a bit. My surging brain is a'weary. I must have some refreshment. Aha, there is a dairy-maid. She can give me a glass of new-laid milk. (*Goes to the booth.*) My dear, a glass of milk.

Marian. For two?

Sheriff. No; for one. This young man has reformed.

Marian. Here you are, sir.

Sheriff. Your health, my dear. Nice girl—very.

Guy. Come, answer my question, Master Sheriff. How am I to win the heart of this Lady Marian with the ten thousand crowns?

Sheriff. Come, I will give you a lesson. You can practice on yon little dairy-maid.

Guy. But is it proper for me—a future peer of England—to waste my time on that sort of people?

Sheriff. Tut! tut! that sort of people frequently waste time upon peers of England.

Guy. Very well; if you say so, I will do the best I can. Only you must freely criticise me.

Sheriff. Criticise you, my boy; I'll show you how it's all done.

TRIO. *Marian, Sheriff and Guy.*

Sheriff.
> When a peer makes love to a damsel fair,
> Before he begins to make his confession,
> He stands statuesquely to make an impression;
> Well, something like this is the proper air.
> Do you think you could do like that, my lad?
> That's very nice—pretty well—not bad.

Guy.
> I'll follow your suggestion,
> And I'll ask the fateful question.

Marian. (*Churning.*)
> Churning, churning,
> All the live-long day;
> Earning, earning
> Wherewithal to pay,
> For a gown of satin rare,
> For a ribbon for my hair;
> Colin surely will declare
> He will love for aye.

Guy.
> Though like a peer I've stood and acted,
> The damsel's thoughts seem quite distracted.

Sheriff.
> Oh, those are the means that the maids employ;
> Before one begins to yield to his pleading
> She has to pretend that she gives little heeding.

She does this kind of thing—with a mien so coy ;
Do not mind little things like this, my boy.
That's what they do when they think they're coy.
Repeat now after me.

(*Sheriff sings and Guy repeats each phrase.*)

Sweetheart, my own sweetheart,
Lift up thy bonny eyes,
And bid with love's fond art
My drooping spirits rise ;
Behold a peer who kneels
Upon his peerless knee,   (*Both kneel.*)
And who distinctly feels
A fiery flame for thee.

Marian.   Well, if for love of me you burn,
Suppose you help me churn.

Sheriff. (*Aside to Guy.*)   Consent.
Guy.   Of course.
Sheriff.   I'll illustrate the art
By which to win her heart.
This is the way to kneel ;
It is the height of grace.

Marian.   How very dreary.
Sheriff.   'Tis thus you try to steal
A miniature embrace.   (*Illustrates.*)

Marian.   He makes me weary.
Sheriff.   When you your love unfold,
Smile pensively this wise.

Marian.   Oh, very fine indeed !
Sheriff.   Hands o'er your heart you hold,
And wildly roll your eyes.

Marian.   Such tactics must succeed.
All.   Burning, yearning
All the live-long day ;
Learning, learning
Love's perplexing way.
Love is darkest of despair,
Love is radiance most rare ;
Love is solace or a care,
Changeable for aye.

(*All exit. Outlaws' horns heard at a distance. Robert, Little John, Scarlet, Allan-a-Dale, Outlaws, Dame Durden, Annabel and Villagers enter.*)

Dame. And who has won the prize, good masters ?
Little J. Who, but young Robert of Huntington ? O, what a pity he is not one of us.

Allan. But nobody should grudge him his good luck. He made a bull's eye at every shot.

Robert. Yes, fortune is kind to me to-day. It is on this day that I come into my title and estates.

Little J. And who is the custodian of your property?

Robert. The Lord High Sheriff of Nottingham. In the absence of the King at the Crusades, this Sheriff's power is absolute ; but I shall make a demand on him at once, and, as I am of age to-day, I do not think he dare refuse.

Little J. Refuse? Let him try it. We'll stand by you ; won't we, boys?

All. Hurrah !

Robert. Come, then. Let's have him out, and as soon as I get possession of my fortune you shall all make merry at my expense.

Friar T. Ah, that's the kind of a nobleman for you. And we're to make merry at his expense. A cheer for him.

All. Hurrah !

(*Robert goes to the door of the Sheriff's house and knocks at the door with the large iron knocker.*)

FINALE.

Robert.	What ho ! Within there !
All.	Within there ! What ho !
Robert.	For you, Lord Sheriff, we await,
	So of our call be heedful ;
	Produce my title and estate,
	Produce the cash so needful.
(*Rapping on the door.*)	Rat-tat-tat-tat. You hear me rap.
	Now come and join us soon, old chap.
All.	Rat-tat-tat-tat. You hear us rap—etc.

(*The Sheriff, Guy and Marian enter.*)

Sheriff.	Come, come. What means this din so loud?
	Disperse, disperse, you noisy crowd.
All.	Disperse? Ho, ho.
Women.	Disperse? Oh, no.
Little J.	A business errand brings us here ;
	And so forbear that haughty sneer.
Scarlet.	Just hearken to our friend's recital,
	And then confer on him his title.
Robert.	Declare me now as Earl.
Sheriff.	No Earl are you, in sooth,
	You vain, presumptuous youth.

Sheriff. (*Speaking through music.*) I find that by your father's will you are not in it.

Robert. Disinherited ?

All. Disinherited ?

Sheriff. Before you were born your father was secretly married to a young peasant girl, who died when the Earl's first child was born. That first born was reared by me. Behold him, the rightful Earl of Huntington (*all laugh derisively*), as these documents fully prove.

Sheriff. This statement's true. You cannot move it ;
Here are the documents to prove it.

Robert. This is some trick mendacious.

Sheriff. Not so : it is veracious.

Guy. Of course I am the real Earl.

Sheriff. Those papers prove his title quite.

(*Aside*). I made them all and know they're right.

Marian (*who holds the order of the King for her marriage to the Earl of Huntington.*)

If this young churl uncouth,
Is Huntington in truth,
I will suppress the King's command ;
I'll not accept his hand.

(*She hides the order of the King in her sun-bonnet.*)

Robert. Traitor ! In the absence of the King your will is law ! But when he returns from the Crusades. I know that he will see justice done.

Little J. And now, friend Robert, take your bow of yew ;
Come to old Sherwood ; join our jolly crew,
Instead of Earl, a monarch you shall be ;
The king of forest rovers, subjects free.

Robert. I take you at your word. Your hand—
Right gladly will I join your band.

Outlaws. Come ! away !
We are most joyful this to see ;
'Tis plain an outlaw he will be.

Robert. Farewell until we meet again. (*To Marian.*)
Farewell to thee ;
Farewell. Although a king I reign ;
Faithful I'll be.

All. Then away let us go to the forest free and fair.
There a king you may be, and a king who has not a care.
Come away ! Come away ! For life is merry there.

(*Robert takes leave of Marian, and is carried off on the shoulders of several of the outlaws, who march off in procession, headed by Little John, Friar Tuck, Will Scarlet and Allan. Curtain.*)

END OF ACT I.

ACT II.

CHORUS.

Oh, cheerily soundeth the huntsman's horn !
   Its clarion blast so fine
Through deeps of old Sherwood is clearly borne ;
We hear it at eve and at break of morn ;
   Of Robin Hood's band the sign.

   A'hunting we will go ;
      (Tra-ra-ra, tra-ra.)   (*Imitating horns.*)
   And chase the hart and roe ;
      (Tra-ra-ra, tra-ra.)
   O, where is band so jolly
      As Robin's band all in Lincoln green ?
   Their life is pleasant folly ;
      None's ever so gay, I ween.

Scarlet.   A tailor there dwelt near old Sherwood's edge,
      Who was deft with an old cross-bow ;
   One day, as he sat on his window ledge,
      That way came a jet black crow.
   He perched on an oak and to caw began—
      One could hear him a'near and far :
   " It takes nine tailors to make a man ;
      A ninth of a man, sir, you are."

Tenors.   " It takes nine tailors"—etc.
Basses.   " Caw, caw, caw"—etc.

Scarlet.   The tailor, he waxed exceeding fierce,
      Crying : " Wife, bring my old crossbow."
   And a cloth-yard shaft he dispatched to pierce
      The heart of that jet black crow.
   But he killed his fav'rite pig as it ran,
      While the crow screamed and flew afar :
   " It takes nine tailors to make a man ;
      A ninth of a man, sir, you are."

Tenors.   " It takes nine tailors"—etc.
Basses.   " Caw, caw, caw, caw"—etc.

(*Annabel enters from the lodge.*)

Little J. A jolly good song and jolly well sung. Come, sweet Annabel.
fill me a tankard of that brown, October ale. (*Annabel presents him
with a tankard which she has filled at the cask.*) Here's to your bonny
black eyes, my dear.

Allan. Come away from him, Annabel You are getting so that you flirt
with every man that comes to the lodge. It is intolerable.

Annabel. And you are getting so that I believe you would be jealous of a
marble statue. (*All laugh.*)

(*Horn outside.*)

Scarlet. That must be our captain.

Little J. Yes ! That is his trumpet.

Friar T. (*who has been cooking the soup*). And he is just in time, for the
soup is all ready. (*Outlaws cheer.*)

(*Robin enters with a deer.*)

Little J. Welcome. Captain ! As usual, you do not return empty-handed.

Robin. No fear of that while the King's preserves are so well stocked.
Sweet Annabel, may I crave a bumper of humming ale from your fair
hands ?

Annabel. Here it is, all ready for you, brave Robin.

Robin. And here's a kiss for your courtesy. (*Kisses her.*)

Allan. Will you never leave off making love to every new-comer ? Do
you think men were made for you to kiss ?

Annabel. Partly for that, I'm sure.

Robin. What, Allan ; are you jealous of Annabel again ? Nonsense, man !

Allan. It may be nonsense, but Annabel is a sad coquette, and I love her
so that she keeps my temper at white heat.

Robin. My regard for her is purely Platonic, and just to prove it, lovely
Annabel, I will come to your window at moonrise this evening. and
sing you a purely Platonic serenade.

Annabel. And I will open my lattice to listen with all the pleasure in life.

Allan. And if you do, all is over between us.

Annabel. It's little I care for that, Master Allan. Come as you say,
Master Robin—just to plague this jealous fellow.

Robin. Not I. I will come to please myself, not to plague him.

Allan. You might not be so much at ease if you knew that the Sheriff of
Nottingham had set forth with a party of foresters sworn to capture the
outlaw, Robin Hood.

Robin. Perhaps ; but the Sheriff does not know that the outlaw, Robin
Hood, and the rightful Earl of Huntington, are one and the same per
son. He thinks that I have gone to the Crusades and have peacefully
yielded up my birthright.

Little J. I knew that such a merry fellow as you would be happier with us.

Robin. Happy? Yes, I am happy, except——

Little J. Excepting when you think of the Lady Marian, eh? Take my advice, man, and don't waste a thought on her.

Friar T. Banish thoughts of love, Captain. and join me in the soup. (*All laugh.*)

Little J. Ho! draw a mug of yonder nappy ale. When an outlaw prates of love and such-like evils, there's but one remedy—a flagon of brown, October ale. Sing the praises of bright eyes and ruddy lips, an ye will. I sing the praise of ale.

THE SONG OF BROWN, OCTOBER ALE.

I.

Little John.

And it's will ye quaff with me, my lads,
　　And it's will ye quaff with me?
It is a draught of nut-brown ale
　　I offer unto ye.
All humming in the tankard, lads,
　　It cheers the heart forlorn;
Oh, here's a friend to ev'ryone—
　　'Tis stout John Barleycorn.

Chorus.

So laugh, lads, and quaff, lads;
　　'Twill make you stout and hale;
Through all my days, I'll sing the praise
　　Of brown, October ale.
Now, tapster, if in me you'd win
　　A friend who will not fail,
Fill up once more the cannikin
　　With brown, October ale.

II.

Little John.

And it's will you love me true, my lass,
　　And it's will you love me true?
If not, I'll drink one flagon more,
　　And so farewell to you.
If Joan or Moll, or Nan or Doll
　　Should make your heart to mourn,
I'll give a friend who will be stanch—
　　'Tis rare John Barleycorn.

Chorus.

So laugh, lads, and quaff, lads,
　　While flagons do not fail,
We'll happy be with three times three
　　Of brown, October ale.

Now, you, good wife, and you good man,
 Let not your mirth grow stale ;
But round we'll pass the clinking can
 Of brown, October ale.

Little John. By my troth, Robin, the cask is empty. I'll challenge you to shoot for a new one.

Robin. I'm your man.

Friar T. And I'll be the umpire   Come on   (*Exit all singing refrain.*)

    Enter Allan, R. 3.

Allan-a-Dale. Oh, my sweet little Annabel. If you would only promise to be faithful to your Allan, and assure me of your trust and constancy, how happy I should be !

    SONG.

    OH, PROMISE ME.

    I.

Oh, promise me that some day you and I
 Will take our love together to some sky
Where we can be alone, and faith renew,
 And find the hollows where those flowers grew.
The first sweet violets of early spring,
 That come in whispers, fill our thoughts,
And sing of love unspeakable that is to be.
  Oh, promise me, oh, promise me.

    II.

Oh, promise me that you will take my hand,
 The most unworthy in this lonely land,
And let me sit beside you —
 In your eyes behold the vision of a paradise,
Hearing God's message, while the organ peals
 Its mighty music to my very soul.
No love less perfect than a life with thee,
  Oh, promise me, oh, promise me.

 (*The Sheriff enters with Guy and six journeymen tinkers.*)

Sheriff. Here we are on the borders of Sherwood Forest, where Robin Hood commits his fearful crimes. (*Sir Guy trembles violently.*) What is the matter with the Earl of Huntington ? If you tremble like that you'll shake down some of these trees You seem to think you have got to be shaken before Robin is taken.

Guy. I'm not afraid of outlaws, but I don't believe in going up to them and asking them to cut your throat as a personal favor.

Sheriff. Sir Guy, I'm afraid you've lost confidence in the massive brain that has brought you to your present rank—just now you are as rank as anybody, and all because I fixed it for you. Marian has fled to

Sherwood Forest. If we don't find her you can't get that ten thousand crowns, and I can't get the ninety thousand. The King has commanded her to marry the Earl of Huntington—that's you. You stick to me, and you will wallow in diamonds.

Guy. But think of Robin Hood. Br-r-r-r (*trembles*).

Sheriff (*imitating him*) What are you doing that for?

Guy (*trembling*). I am quaking at the dread name of Robin Hood. They say he sticks at nothing

Sheriff. I don't care if he sticks at everything Robin Hood never robs from the poor—sensible man : they have nothing worth taking. As journeymen tinkers we are too poor to attract his attention. Perhaps we will get a chance to capture this Robin, whoever he may be. You seem to forget that I have my eagle eye with me.

Guy. Which is your eagle eye?

Sheriff. The left—and there's no hypermetropic blendicular conjunctivitis about it. Trust to my colossal intellect, friend Guy, and we will not only bring Marian back so you can marry her, but we will hang Robin on a highly ornate and commodious gallows.

Guy. Yes ; but if we are journeymen tinkers, we had better attend to business.

Sheriff. True, we must keep up our characters. Who knows but Robin Hood may be in this very lodge. Come, to work, my honest journeymen, and, like all true craftsmen, beguile your toil with blithe roundelay.

TINKER'S SONG.

I.

'Tis merry journeymen we are.
All in the tinkering line, sirs ;
We tramp the roadways near and far,
If weather it be fine, sirs.
And if so be some churlish lout
Should make us surly answers,
We straightway drown his utterance out
By tapping on our pans, sirs.
Then we rap, rap, rap,
And we tap, tap, tap,
From the dawn till the dark of night, sirs ;
We are men of mettle,
And the can or kettle
Doesn't live that we can't set right, sirs.
Tink tank, clink clank—
Hear our hammers ring ;
When trade is brisk
We frolic and we frisk
As happy and gay as a king.

23

II.

Your tinker is a blithesome blade,
    A cheerful soul I wot, sirs ;
And gin enow he be not paid,
    He thieves what you have got, sirs.
He tells the news from town to town,
    The true news and the lie, sirs ;
You'll search the whole world up and down
    And find no wight so sly, sirs.
        () we rap, rap, rap—etc.

(Robin, Little John, Friar Tuck, Scarlet and Annabel enter. Annabel serves ale to the Sheriff.)

Friar T. Don't run so fast down hill. Come ; what say you to a game of skittles ?

Little J. I'll lay you a stoup of sack that I can beat you, my fat friar.

Scarlet. How now, thou roystering boaster ! I'll cast a bowl with you right willingly. Now, what say you to this ? *(Bowls)*

Friar T. All down, but seven !

Sheriff. I wonder who these rapscallions are. Do you know these noisy wights, sweet damsel ?

Annabel. *(Aside.)* I must not betray such good customers. *(To the Sheriff.)* Know them ? Ay, marry.

Sheriff. Oh, you marry, do you ? Which one ?

Annabel. Methinks they are a party of yeomen sent by the King to capture Robin Hood.

Sheriff. *(Slightly tipsy.)* Bah ! What can yeomen do ? They lack shrewdness, sagacious-ness-ness ; eagle-eye tiveness. They have not an eagle eye to their backs.

Annabel. *(Aside to Robin.)* Beware, brave Robin, or you will not sing that serenade to me this night. Yonder fellow is the Sheriff of Nottingham come to capture you.

Robin and the Outlaws. *(Aside.)* The Sheriff !

Little J. *(To the Sheriff.)* Look ye, my lusty tinkers, have you heard the sad news from Banbury ?

Sheriff (maudlin). Sad news from Cranberry ? What's the sad news ? Tell me, for I am a tinker by trade and as greedy for news as a priest is for farthings.

Scarlet. Yes ; it is said that two tinkers have been placed in the stocks for drinking small beer.

Sheriff. A plague on thy news, thou scurvy loon. Thou speakest ill of my trade.

Little J. But the sad news is, there are but two tinkers in the stocks, the others still roam the country.

Sheriff. Now, by the pewter platter of Saint Dunstan, I've a mind to baste thine hide for that ill-mannered jest.

Robin. Tut, tut, jolly menders of kettles. You see we are four stout yeomen to two tinkers ; so for our own sakes let us not fall to cracking crowns.

Friar T. No, but fall to cracking jests over a stoup of sack.

Little J. Ho, my sweet Annabel. Bring us to drink.

Sheriff. I do love you as brothers all, else would I not waste time with ye : for I am a sly dog, and I have in my pocket a warrant for that villainous outlaw, Robin Hood.

Little J. Thou hast a warrant ?

Sheriff. Ay, here in this pouch.

Guy. Yes ; and we seek also the Lady Marian Fitzwalter, who is ordered by the King to marry the Earl of Huntington—that is I.

Robin. Lady Marian to marry you ?

Little J. (*Aside.*) Tut, tut ! I will attend to this. (*To the Sheriff.*) And where is this fair dame ?

Sheriff. Troth, she has fled from home and gone we know not whither.

Robin. (*Aside.*) Can she have come to the forest to join me ? (*Returns to the table.*)

Sheriff. My first business must be to serve this warrant upon Robin Hood. An' he mind it not I will cudgel him till every one of his bones cries out amen. But mayhap some of ye know this Robin.

Little J. Know him ? Not we, indeed ! But drink, man ; drink.

(*Little John makes the Sheriff drink and pretends to drink himself. The other outlaws pretend to drink and laugh aside at the Sheriff.*)

Friar T. (*To Guy.*) Drink, sweet youth ; drink.

Sheriff. (*Drinking.*) I'll catch this vagabond Robin and hang him on the highest gallows in merry England.

Robin. (*Aside.*) The old villain !

Scarlet. Here's a health to you, my fine fellow.

(*Sheriff drinks. Scarlet pretends to drink and throws the ale on the ground.*)

Little J. But, tinker, they say this Robin Hood is a sly thief.

Sheriff. What do I care ? So am I—I mean I'm sly.

Little J. You had better watch your warrant closely, or he may steal it. (*Little John takes the warrant from the Sheriff's pouch.*)

Sheriff. Steal it ? Ho, ho ! That's a joke. Steal from me ? Let him try it.

Little J. He'd only have to try it ; wouldn't he ? Ho, ho, ho ! (*All laugh.*)

Sheriff. Oh, if I only had him here. man to man.

Little J. He'd show you ; wouldn't he ?

Guy. But what manner of man is Robin Hood ?

Robin. I saw him once. He is much such a man as I.

Little J. (*Aside.*) Take care. You will betray yourself.

Sheriff. Egad ! I thought him a bearded and blear-eyed ruffian ; but if he be a young churl like you, so much the easier task to crack his knave's pate.

Robin. What say you?

Scarlet. (*Aside.*) Hold, Robin, be patient with the villain.

Robin. Perchance, master tinker, this Robin is a deft hand with a cudgel.

Sheriff. Deft he may be ; but I am defter.

Little J. Then quaff another tankard.

Sheriff. Not I ; always know when to stop. (*He is the worse for liquor.*) I must keep my eagle eye and my immense brain in good working order. Not another drop.

Scarlet. (*To Guy.*) Have a round with me, young friend ?

Guy. No more ; I must keep perfectly straight.

Sheriff. (*Trying to rise with dignity.*) I am afraid I have taken about a teaspoonful too much.

Little J. Nonsense, man ! We are getting jolly together. Look at me. I am worse than you.

Friar T. I am the worst of all of ye.

Sheriff. So you are. Here, give me another tankard. I allow no man to be worse than I am.

Little J. Why, master tinker, you are as sober as a judge. How do you manage to do it?

Sheriff. Do it by—great eye—eagle brain. (*Falls into the chair.*)

Friar T. And now, what say all of you to a song ?

All. A song, a song !

Sheriff. Song? I'faith, in singing I can beat you all. I have the loudest voice in all the country round.

Guy. I can't sing with you, for I know no songs.

Friar T. Oh, you must all join in. I have a right jolly song here, writ by myself. Hearken, and keep your eyes upon these same notes.

(*Gives out parts of a song which he takes from his pockets.*)

Tranquilo cum Friskioso:

PASTORAL GLEE.

All.
O, see the lambkins play,
The birdlings pipe on every tree ;
The kids do frisk right gladsomelie ;
And bleat the lambs
Beside their dams,
They are so full of glee.
Yes, they are full——
They are so full——
They are so full of glee.

Friar T. Oh, dear——

Little J. Oh, dear.——

Sheriff. Oh, dear——

All. Oh, dear Aminta, come with me.

Friar T. Oh, dam——

Sheriff.	Oh, dam——
Scarlet.	Oh, dam——
All.	Oh, damsel fair, spring is wintry without thee.
Friar T.	Now swear——
Sheriff.	Now swear——
All.	Now swear I need not doubt thee.
Friar T.	Oh, pay, my fair——
Sheriff.	Oh, pay, my fair——
All.	Oh, pay, my fair, this love of mine,
	I cannot live without thee.

The frogs right wantonly do sing ;
The daffodils do bloom and spring.
    If my Aminta doth deny
    To hear my love-lorn sigh,

Friar T.	I'll seek my bier——
Sheriff.	I'll seek my bier——
All.	I'll seek my lonely bier to die.

Young Strephon loves her too ;
    He is so sly ;

Friar T.	So black his eye——
Scarlet.	So black his eye——
All.	So black is his roguish eye.

Aminta hear and make reply,
Or bid me seek my bier to die.

SEXTETTE.

Little J.	When lads have had enow,
	Song is most meet, I trow
Sheriff (*sleepy at the table*).	(Fol-di-riddle, fol-di-row.)
Scarlet.	Timid hearts braver are ;
	Bold hearts are bolder far.
Sheriff.	(Fol-di-riddle, fol-di-row.)
All.	Ho then for jollity,
	Fun and frivolity ;
	Drink with avidity,
	Banish timidity ;
	Try the experiment,
	'Twill bring you merriment.
	Quaff with me.
	Laugh with me.
	Jolly dogs we.

(*All dance off but the Sheriff. Dame Durden enters.*)

Dame. What's this ? All gone. And who is to pay for the six quarterns of good malt liquor they had ? Ah ; they have left one of the tinkers here—the worse for liquor. too. Come, sir tinker. You owe me ten good shillings for the ale you have had.

Sheriff. What's that ? What's tha· ?

Dame. Come ; you are not too drunk to pay me ten shillings.

Sheriff. I pay nothing ! Great eye—eagle brain—never pay for anything.

Dame. (*Aside.*) If I can find his purse, I will pay myself. How now ! He hath no purse. He hath nothing but this letter. (*Takes letter from the Sheriff's pocket.*) Merciful powers ! what do I see ? My letter !

Sheriff. Letter ! What letter ?

Dame. It is the letter that I sent to my husband at the Crusades ; and the same suit of homespun. Can this be gaffer Durden, my own long-lost husband ? For twelve long years I have not seen you. The campaigns have changed you sadly, but your figure and height are the same. Oh, what joy to see you again. (*Embraces him.*)

Sheriff. Egad ! I seem to have won the fancy of this buxom dame. Madam, I prithee, hold off and unhand me unless your intentions be honorable, for I am a discreet and prudent bachelor.

Dame. And do you love me still, my own hubby ?

Sheriff. Hubby ? Hubby ? Well, don't get gay with hubby.

Dame. Certainly. Are you not my liege lord ?

Sheriff. Woman, aroint ! and get you gone ! I am liege lord to no dame ; but I am a discreet and prudent bachelor. The taint of scandal has never bruised my fair 'scutcheon.

Dame. What, you deny your own wife ?

Sheriff. I tell you I have no wife.

Dame. Villain, after your leaving me for twelve years ; after my sending you a suit of homespun every year, you have the face to deny me ?

Sheriff. You have a face that *makes* me deny you. If you have a grand-daughter, I will talk business ; but I am not in need of a grandmother's care.

Dame. I will appeal to the Sheriff of Nottingham. He will put you in the stocks.

Sheriff (*falling on his knees*). No, no ! Anything but that ! Don't tell the Sheriff. If he should fix his igle eeye on me, I would be lost. The Noriff of Sheringham is one of the greatest men of the age.

Dame. One of the greatest fools !

Sheriff. What's that ? What's that ?

Dame. But he hath wit enow to deal with you.

Sheriff. Now, my aged but worthy crone, do you mean to say that I am married to you ?

Dame. Certainly. Have I not been a faithful wife to you for twenty years ?

Sheriff. Well, not that I am aware of.

Dame. Did I not send you the very clothes you wear—made by these hands ?

Sheriff. These clothes ?

Dame. To be sure. If you deny that you came by them lawfully you must be a thief ; so when I drag you before the Sheriff, he will have your right hand cut off for stealing.

Sheriff. (*Aside.*) I see. It's all on account of these clothes I bought at auction. I must humor her, or I will be arrested for buying stolen goods. As Sheriff it would be my duty to arrest myself and have my right hand cut off (*To her.*) Ha ! ha ! I was only joking with you. Of course you are my wife, and a better wife I don't remember ever having married.

Dame. Ah, at last he recognizes me. (*Embraces him.*)

Sheriff. (*Aside.*) I fancy that was rather clever of me. (*To her.*) Recognize you ? Of course I do. It's a wise man that knows his own wife.

Dame. But come within and I will give you something to banish the effects of drinking overmuch. You shall have a rasher of bacon. You must be hungry after twelve years.

Sheriff. Yes ; a twelve years' fast *has* put an edge on my appetite. (*Aside.*) The old beldame thinks that I've had nothing to eat for twelve years. Well, a fast of twelve years has put an edge on my appetite ! Come, let's within and have that basher of racon—I mean that rasher of bacon.

Dame. And you shall have a steak, too.

Sheriff. A steak ! Well, here goes another martyr to the steak.

(*She drags the Sheriff into the house* R. *Marian enters dressed in a hunting costume of Lincoln green.*)

Marian. In Sherwood Forest at last. The Sheriff insists upon my marriage with Guy of Gisbone, but it shall never be, for I have come to join Robin Hood and his merry men.

SOLO. *Marian.*

'Neath greenwood trees
All Nature is at peace and rest ;
Each bird that warbles from its nest
Tells me of one whom I love best.
Yon bright brooklet gleaming
With greeting, too, is teeming.
Long have I been dreaming
  Of the hour we two should meet,

Ye birds, in azure winging,
I thank you for your singing.
  Tidings from my love you bring afar.
Ev'ry blossom seems to tell me he is true ;
His voice is echoed by the streamlet blue.

I seem to hear
My love's voice near,
Echoed by the breezes blowing,
And the brooklet in its flowing—
All these voices say he is near.
Ye birds in azure winging,
I thank ye for your singing.
Yes, ev'ry song that's ringing
Is a tender token bringing
From the one·who is nearest, dearest ;
Yes, they tell me he is near.

(*Annabel enters from the house.*)

Annabel. Whom have we here ? A new recruit for Robin Hood's band ?

Marian. You have guessed the truth, my good girl. I have come to join Robin Hood.

Annabel. Oh, I suppose you are a sweetheart of his ?

Marian. Certainly I am.

Annabel. Then what right has Robin Hood to make love to me ?

Marian. He makes love to you, does he ? (*Aside.*) Faithless wretch !

Annabel. The most desperate love. This very evening he promised to come and sing beneath my window.

Marian. Fine doings, truly. And you, I suppose, promised to open your lattice to him.

Annabel. To be sure, I did.

Marian. But is there no sweetheart to whom you are particularly true ?

Annabel. Yes, young Allan-a-Dale, of Robin Hood's band. He is a gallant lad, only he is terribly jealous. Only think, he says if I see Robin Hood this night, all is over between us. It was that which decided me to see Robin.

Marian. Just for the sake of getting you out of this scrape with Robin, I will keep the appointment that you have with him. Thus you can remain good friends with your Allan and I will surprise Robin, who seeks to play me false.

Annabel. I agree.

Marian. Mind ; I only do this as a favor to you.

Annabel. Come, then, and I will show you my room. When your Robin appears below the window, you can open the lattice to him in my stead.

Marian (*with affected indifference*). Oh, very well ; I follow you.

(*Annabel leads the way into the house. Marian continues, as she follows Annabel.*) I hope that the moonlight will be bright enough for Robin to see my face. (*Exits.*)

(Guy enters, followed by Allan-a-Dale.)

Guy. Master Sheriff! Master Sheriff! Oh, where can he be? Master Sheriff!

Allan. Yes, call him forth, and I will play the traitor with a right good will. Come forth, Master Sheriff, an you would capture the outlaw, Robin Hood.

(Sheriff appears in doorway of the house.)

Sheriff. That woman is a good soul if she does say she is my wife. She gave me some herb tea and seething soorup and I feel as well as ever. Hello, friend Guy, what do you want?

Guy. Here is a golden opportunity. This is one of Robin Hood's band who wants to give Robin up to justice.

Sheriff. Where is this true-hearted and gentlemanly outlaw?

Allan. I am the man.

Sheriff. So you are anxious to give up Robin, are you? I think this is rather clever of me. At what price, eh?

Allan. Price! At no price! I give him up as I would give up the whole band, if they played me such a trick. I want no money.

Sheriff. (*Aside.*) So much the better. I will charge it up to the county as paid to him, and put the money—well, never mind. (*To Allan.*) Young man, it does you credit; you are not a traitor for revenue only.

Allan. The villain.

Sheriff. But what are you giving Robin up for?

Allan. Because he is trying to rob me of my sweetheart, Annabel. I cannot live without her. Rather than see her marry him, I will deliver him up to the Sheriff.

Sheriff. That's right. Now, just fancy Robin printing a kiss upon her beautiful lips.

Allan. Oh, the villain!

Sheriff. You can't think of his arm around her slim waist without squirming with anguish.

Guy. Think of her snow-white arms about his neck.

Allan. Perdition!

Sheriff. Perdition? I should say so. Now, where can we find him, eh?

Allan. Meet me here at moonrise and I will point him out to you.

Guy. But will you surely be here?

Allan. Indeed I will be here to gloat over his capture.

Sheriff. You need not trouble yourself about doing any gloating. If any gloating is necessary, I can attend to it. As a gloater, I am a shining success.

Guy. Noble young man. Take this purse of gold for your trouble.

Allan. I do not want your money. Vengeance is enough for me. (*Throws down purse. Exits.*)

Sheriff. If you tried to pay your board with vengeance, you would not find it go very far. What did I tell you, friend Guy? You stick to me and you will be inlaid with cash. Come now, let us tell our jovial tinkers to be in readiness.

Guy. Yes, we will need their help. There is one of him and only six of us.

Sheriff. What care we for numbers? We would get the best of him if we were twice as many.

(*Guy and the Sheriff exit. During this scene the stage has grown darker and the moon rises. Robin enters.*)

Robin. Oh, Marian, Marian, if I could only believe you true. But did not Guy of Gisborne himself say that she was to marry him? Yes, it was the King's command she should marry the Earl of Huntington, as he now calls himself. She is lost to me forever. But I must not forget that I was to sing a serenade to that little coquette, Annabel. At least, she has the merit of not pretending to be true to anyone.

SOLO. *Robin.*

I.

A troubadour sang to his love,
Who looked from her lattice on high :
" So long as the moon shines above,
So long will I be
Ever faithful to thee,
So long as the moon's in the sky.
The moon must shine for aye ;
So hear my roundelay."
'Twas thus sang blithely the troubadour :
And his melody cast a spell ;
For the damsel hearkened and loved him more
Than ever a damsel might tell.

II.

At day, when the moon was asleep,
That troubadour warbled his lay
To other fair ladies who weep,
Who pensively sigh
And softly reply,
Who vow they will love him for aye.
He only vowed to love
While Luna shone above ;
So did not faithless prove.
Thus sang he ever, that troubadour,
And his melody cast a spell ;
For the damsels hearkened and loved him more
Than ever young damsels might tell.

(*Marian enters from house wearing Annabel's red cloak. Moonlight. Marian keeps her face averted from Robin.*)

Marian.   So, gallant Robin, thou dost bring
            This serenade to me to sing?
Robin.   No serenade could ever tell
            How much I love thee, and how well.

(*Allan, followed by Scarlet, appears. Scarlet trying to restrain Allan, who is angry on seeing Marian, whom he mistakes for Annabel.*)

Allan.   (*Aside.*)   She is false to me, the jade.
Scarlet. (*Aside.*)   Pray be calm and undismayed.
Marian.   (*Aside.*)   I am forgotten, I'm afraid.
Robin.   No serenade could ever tell
                             How much I love sweet Annabel.
Allan.   (*Aside.*)   Her scorn I will repay.
Marian.   (*Aside.*)   He has a winning way.
Robin.   (*Aside.*)   She shall not say me nay.
Scarlet. (*To Allan, aside.*) I pray thee think of her no more.
                             Some other girl adore.
Robin and Marian.   Yes, yes, I love thee. I own.
                             My heart is thine alone.
Allan.   (*Aside.*)   My vengeance she shall know.
                             Shall she wed him? Nay, not so.
                             She shall be mine alone.
Scarlet.   We must no longer stay.
                             I prithee come away. (*Scarlet forces Allan away.*)

Robin. Ah, my little Annabel, with you I may cease to remember that there are high-born ladies who forget their vows and foreswear their loves.

Marian. (*Turning her face toward him.*) Is there any particular high-born lady to whom you refer, Master Robin?

Robin. (*Amazed.*) It is Marian.

Marian. Yes, your injured and deserted Marian. I have heard of your pranks with village girls, and with shame I confess that I love one whom I find engaged in singing rapturous love songs to another.

Robin. Forgive me, Marian, I thought you false. Rumor says that you are to marry Guy of Gisborne, who has usurped my title, my estates.

Marian. Yes; and it was to prevent such a marriage that I have come to link my fortunes with yours.

Robin. Oh, that's very well for a jest, my girl; but it is impossible—excepting on one condition.

(*Sheriff, Guy, Allan and two tinkers enter. They listen to the following dialogue. Allan angry at seeing Robin with one whom he supposes to be Annabel.*)

Marian. And what may that be?

Robin. Consent to our immediate marriage.

Allan. (*Aside.*) Marriage!

Robin. Friar Tuck can marry us as safe and sound as a bishop.

Marian. Very well, I accept the condition.

Robin. And the jolly Friar shall marry us on the morrow.

Allan. (*Aside.*) Annabel marry Robin? It shall never be. Seize him!

Robin. Allan-a-Dale a traitor! I cannot believe it. (*Tinkers seize Robin.*)

Sheriff. What? My ward, Marian?

Allan. Not Annabel? O Captain!

Marian. Yes, I have come to join Robert.

Sheriff. Robert, say you?

Marian. Yes; the rightful Earl of Huntington, whom you have driven
to get an honest living by highway robbery.

Sheriff. Robin Hood and Robert of Huntington the same!

Robin. Yes; the terrible brigand you have been hunting for months, who
has robbed the rich and befriended the poor; who has slain the King's
deer and fought the King's men, is none other than Robert of Huntington.

Sheriff. So much the better. Seize him! Oh, you are seizing him. Well,
you other fellows seize him too. He is a terrible creature. Now on to
Nottingham town!

Marian. You shall not take him without me.

Sheriff. That's all right, my dear. We are going to take you, never fear.
Come. Away with them. She to the altar—he to the halter. Ha, ha,
ha! My eagle eye triumphs!

Robin. Stop! One moment, my crafty friend. You have played all your
trumps, but I have one left.

Sheriff. (*Dismayed.*) The deuce!

Robin. The deuce? Perhaps not; it may be the King. (*Sounds his horn.*)

(*The Outlaws rush on, led by Allan. Little J, Scarlet and Friar Tuck enter
with the others. Little J. and Scarlet release Robin. Friar Tuck ties the
Sheriff's arms behind him.*)

Allan. Captain, it was I who brought about your capture; but I have also
effected your release.

Robin. I forgive you for the one and thank you for the other. I thank
you one and all, brave comrades.

Friar T. Here is our arch-enemy, the Sheriff. I surrounded him all by
myself.

Little J. What shall we do with the Sheriff?

All. Hang him.

Sheriff. Gentlemen, I beg that you will not hang me while I have this bad
cold. It would be cruelty.

(*Dame Durden enters.*)

Dame. My poor, dear husband, what are these men doing to you?

Little J. Husband?

All. Her husband?

Sheriff. Woman, get you gone and let these gentlemen hang me in peace. Haven't I enough trouble without your persisting that you are my wife?

Little J. Do you mean to say that you are this man's wife?

Dame. Certainly ; that is as near as I can tell. He has been away from me for twelve long years, but his figure is the same.

Sheriff. Oh, my figure's the same. I wish I hadn't brought it with me.

Little J. Speak, man ; are you this woman's husband?

Sheriff Do I look like a collector of antiquities?

Scarlet. Don't evade the question, but tell the truth.

Sheriff. How can I be her husband, when she's not my wife?

Dame. Oh, the old villain!

All. Oh, the old villain !

Dame. Then tell me, you rascal, how did you come by this suit of clothes that you have on?

Sheriff. I bought them at an auction sale.

Dame. That is false ; I made them with my own hands. *(Produces letter.)* And this letter I found in his pocket even now.

Robin. Now, if you are not this honest woman's husband, how did you get this suit of homespun and this letter?

Allan. *(Aside to Little J.)* It's the suit we sold at auction at Nottingham.

Dame. If he denies that he is my husband, I denounce him as a thief.

All He's a thief ! Hang him !

Sheriff. Mercy ! Mercy !

Robin. We are honest outlaws, who hold thieving in abhorrence. We show no mercy to thieves.

Dame. You have your choice. Admit that I am your wife or that you are a thief.

Sheriff. Life is very precious to me, and there is a suspense about hanging which is unpleasant—but, I admit that I am a thief.

Little J. He admits his guilt ; to the stocks with him.

All. To the stocks with him.

FINALE.

(The Sheriff is put in the stocks.)

Principals.	Put the Sheriff in the stocks-
All.	In the stocks.
Principals.	For at us he jibes and mocks—
All.	Jibes and mocks.
Outlaws.	In Sherwood's forest the merriest of lives
	Is our life so fair and free,
	And this old hypocrite in gyves
	Made fast shall straightway be.

We'll laugh—ha, ha !—'tis jolly fun
To see him now.
We'll laugh—ha, ha '—the Sheriff is undone ;
And yet, done up, we vow.

All. Look at him, look at him. What a plight.
Certainly he is a gruesome sight.
Prithee, Master Sheriff,
Prithee come away.
Stocks are most becoming
To you we must say.

All. Look at him, look at him. What a plight. (*Etc.*)

Dame. So now, false one, you're in a gruesome plight ;
If you'd acknowledge me I'd aid your flight.

Sheriff. (*Dolefully.*) Woman, get thee gone
And let me die alone.

(*Aside.*) If Guy would come with the King's men,
I'd turn the tables on them then.

Robin. Come, now let's to our forest lair ;
Of ambuscades we must beware.

Little J. Yes ; let's away, for danger's lurking near.

Scarlet. The foresters may find their Sheriff here.

(*From all sides come the King's archers, led by Guy. All the archers draw their bows and level arrows at the Outlaws.*)

Outlaws. We're lost ! We're lost !
Archers. We triumph ! Huzzah !
Guy. Let a man stir and straight his life is done.
We're brave as lions, for we're two to one.

(*The Sheriff is released from the stocks.*)

Sheriff. It seems I have the best of it
Where erst I had the worst ;
Who laughs the last laughs louder far
Than he who laughs the first.
Now, Robin Hood shall go with us,
To Nottingham goes he ;
Sing hey for the merry stocks and chains,
Sing hey for the gallows tree.

All. The very merry,
Heigh down derry,
Rollicking gallows tree.

Marian. But you must set him free,
That he may wed with me.
I'd have you understand
It is the King's command.

Sheriff.   You're dreadfully mistaken, Miss,
         For *he* is not the one.
      The King's command is that she wed
         The Earl of Huntington.
      The Earl of Huntington is Guy,
         And Guy must bridegroom be.
      Sing hey for the merry stocks and chains,
         And the rollicking gallows tree.

All.   The very merry,
         Heigh down derry,
      Rollicking gallows tree.

Robin.   'Tis true. Alas, too true.
Marian.   And I must part from you. ,
Sheriff.   Take them away. To Nottingham let's hie.
      This is a triumph for my eagle eye.

Marian and Robin. Fear not, my darling,
      Hope's bright star may still be shining ;
         Fear not, my love,
      For ev'ry cloud has silver lining.
      I will be true, but come what may,
      The King's command we must obey.

All.   Yes, come what will and come what may,
      The King's command all must obey.

END OF THE SECOND ACT.

ACT III.

SCENE.—*The courtyard of the Sheriff's house. A chapel. A shed in which is a blacksmith's forge with fire. A prison near which is an anvil, before which Will Scarlet is at work making a sword.*

ARMORER'S SONG. *Will Scarlet.*

I.

Let hammer on anvil ring, ring, ring,
    And the forge fire brightly shine ;
Let the wars rage still, while I work with a will
    At this peaceable trade of mine.
The sword is a weapon to conquer fields ;
    I honor the man who shakes it ;
But naught is the lad who the broadsword wields
    Compared to the lad who makes it.
Huzzah for the anvil, the forge and the sledge ;
    Huzzah for the sparks that fly ;
If I had a cup I would straightway pledge
    The armorer—that is I.

        Clang, clang, clang !
      Let carking care go hang.
        Let the trusty sledge
        On the anvil's edge
      By a lusty arm be hurled.
        Cling, cling, cling !
      Let the armorer blithely sing ;
        For it's here is made
        The hero's blade
      That may conquer all the world.

II.

Let others of glory sing, sing, sing,
    As they struggle in glory's quest.
Let them wave their brands in their mailèd hands
    While the sword smites shield and crest.
The soldier's a lad who is stanch and leal,
    And his calling is most glorious ;
But who is it gives him the trusty steel
    That can render him victorious ?

> Huzzah for the wight who can fashion a blade
> That can make a traitor fly :
> Huzzah for the lad who this broadsword made,
> The armorer—that is I.
> Clang, clang, clang !—etc.

(Little John, Friar Tuck and Allan-a-Dale enter, dressed as monks.)

Scarlet. So these are the chains for Robin Hood None would think, to look at them, that I have made them weak in a certain link, so that our Captain may break them at will. Methinks I am well-nigh sly enow for a sheriff. Hello ! Whom have we here ?

Little J. Friend, we are three pious pilgrims who are begging our way from door to door. Perchance thou hast a few crumbs of bread for us.

Allan. Or a few crumbs of sponge cake—

Friar T. Or a few crumbs of cranberry pie—

Little J., Allan and Friar T. Ho! ho! ho ! *(Laughing at Scarlet.)*

Scarlet. Think not to befool me with your cowls and gowns. I know ye too well.

Little J. And how fares the rescue of our Captain?

Scarlet. Methinks all will be well. The Sheriff has planned to have Robin brought from jail to-day that he may witness the marriage of Maid Marian to Guy of Gisborne. "Who will make strong chains for Robin?" quoth the Sheriff. "I am an armorer," said I. Not knowing me to be Will Scarlet, he took me at my word, and here are the chains. *(Friar Tuck tries to break the chains, which all examine)* Be careful, man. You will break them

Little J. Break them ? Ho ! ho ! A fine armorer, truly.

Scarlet. Yes, they are made weak in a certain link, so our Captain may free himself right easily.

Allan. And Annabel? Have you learned anything of her ?

Scarlet. Annabel is to be married to the Sheriff at the same time that Marian is wedded to Guy of Gisborne.

Allan. This is more of her treachery.

Scarlet. No ; blame her not. She is forced into the marriage by Dame Durden, her mother.

Little J. A double wedding, eh? Oh, very well ; then we must have a double rescue. Let us carry off Robin, Marian and Annabel all together.

Scarlet. First I will put on Robin his new chains, which he may easily break.

Little J. The Friar and I will go to Robin's cell to give him spiritual counsel.

Friar T. I'll change clothes with him, and Robin shall come forth in my cowl and gown. I will remain in the cell in his place.

Allan. But the Sheriff will hang you for helping Robin to escape.

Friar T. Hang me? Let him try it. I am a churchman, and sacred from the touch of such profane beasts as sheriffs. Hang me? Let him dare to lay a finger on me, and I will excommunicate him.

Little J. I have brought with me a score of our yeomen, who will rush to aid us at a blast from my bugle.

Allan. And I will seek Annabel, and tell her that at the last moment she may be rescued from her ancient bridegroom. (*Runs off.*)

Scarlet. Now into the jail with me.

Little J. And I would like to see the Sheriff when he comes to look for his prisoner. He will find him so reformed that he has become a pious and holy monk.

(Scarlet, Friar Tuck and Little John enter the jail.)

(Enter Annabel, R. 3.)

Annabel. Oh, this hateful marriage! Is there no way that I can escape it? On her wedding day a girl's thoughts should be only of her future husband. But I cannot, will not think of that wretched old Sheriff. No! All my thoughts are of Allan. Surely he will forgive me and save me from this marriage.

SONG. Annabel.

I.

A maiden's thoughts on her merry wedding day
    Should ever be of love alone.
'Tis not so with me, I'm unhappy as can be,
    And doleful dreams my thoughts employ.
For though I may not wed the one I love,
    Nor evermore his face may see,
Alas! Ah me! Would he were here to save me,
    He's all the world to me.

Then come what may,
My heart is Allan's,
He's the one I love,
And shall love for aye.
Then come what may,
Through all I love him,
In a proper way,
As a maiden may.
He's all the world to me.

II.

Now take warning, maids, if ye marry otherwise
    Than for fond love, for love alone,
Cupid e'er has been such a jealous little sprite
    That lovers all his sway must own.

So wed no old or crusty, fusty fellow,
For the step you will regret.
There's sure to be some young and handsome swain,
Whom you can never quite forget.
Then come what may, etc.

(*The Sheriff and Guy enter, l.. Both are in their wedding clothes.*)

Sheriff. What did I tell you, friend Guy? Did I not say that you would
win the girl if you would trust to my colossal mind and unequaled
eagleness of eye?

Guy. You did indeed, and if you ever want a friend——

Sheriff (interrupting). I don't—they're too expensive. I must be satisfied with gratitude, friend Guy, (*aside*) and with the lion's share of
Robert's estate and Marian's dowry.

Guy. But where is my lovely bride, Marian?

Sheriff. And where is my beauteous little Annabel. I finally persuaded
her mother that I was not her father—I mean that I was not her husband—I mean that I was not Dame Durden's husband, so the Dame
eagerly accepted me as a son-in-law. But where is Annabel?

(*Dame Durden, dragging Annabel, enters. Allan enters, still wearing his
monk's cowl and gown.*) Ha! Here she is, the fairest of her sex—with
a few trifling exceptions. (*To Annabel.*) One little ante-nuptial
embrace. Oh, I doat upon her! (*Goes to Annabel and offers to kiss
her.*)

Annabel (shrinking). Oh, I wish I had an antidote——

Sheriff. Kissing between persons who have plaught—I mean plighted
their troth is not altogether prohibited.

Guy. It's quite the usual thing, you know.

Sheriff. Just a pocket edition of a kiss upon those pearly lips—I mean
ruby lips.

(*Allan steps between Annabel and the Sheriff. The Sheriff, not noticing that
Allan has taken the place of Annabel, kisses him.*)

Sheriff. What impudence is this? To the stocks with this fellow. Take
his measure for a new stocks at once.

Allan. Surely you would not do violence to a poor mendicant monk?

Sheriff. Certainly, if he comes monking around my bride.

(*Robin, wearing Friar Tuck's cowl and gown, and Little John, still as a monk,
enter from the jail. Friar Tuck appears in the window of the jail.*)

Allan. (Aside.) It is I, Allan. (*To the Sheriff.*) I only come, my Lord
Sheriff, to say that the Bishop of Hereford has been captured by Robin
Hood's men, and he is their prisoner in Sherwood Forest.

Dame. The Bishop taken captive!

Annabel. Then the wedding will have to be put off. Oh, joy!

Sheriff. My bonny bride is not wildly anxious to be married. There is nothing of the fever of impatience about Annabel. Courage, my darling. If the Bishop cannot get here to officiate at the double wedding, we will get some pious friar to perform the ceremony. Perhaps this young monk would do. Young man, what terms will you make to marry two couples? A couple of couples, you know; you ought to do it cheaply, you know.

Allan. I would not presume to take the place of the Lord Bishop of Hereford, but I can get you a good churchman who will do it for you.

Robin. What would ye, brethren? A holy man to marry ye? In good sooth, there is no better marrier than I in all Nottinghamshire. Is it not so, Brother Bartholomew?

Little J. Marry, 'tis full of truth that thou sayest, Brother Joseph. Marrying is his specialty, I wot.

Guy. What say you, Master Sheriff? Are you willing this good Friar should take the place of the Bishop?

Sheriff. I would prefer the Bishop; but since my lovely Annabel is restlessly eager to call me hers, the Friar will have to do for us.

Little J. And he *will* do for you. (*Aside.*)

Sheriff. Yonder is the chapel. Mind that you be not late, for the ceremony is soon to begin. We only await one of the brides, and the organ blower.

Little J. Oh, we will be here betimes, never fear.

Robin. Come, Brother Bartholomew.

Little J. Ay, ay, Brother Joseph; but go slowly, for I am sore stricken in years, and my aged form is bent like a forest oak.

(*Robin exits, followed by Little John.*)

Annabel. (*Aside.*) Oh, Allan, forgive me and save me. I only love you; I swear it. (*Church bells ring.*)

Allan. (*Aside.*) Do not fear. Keep up your courage, and at the last moment you and Marian shall be restored to us.

Sheriff (*turning to Allan and Annabel*). How now, my bridey? bridey? Are you trying to captivate this young churchman on your wedding day?

Allan. Calm yourself, Master Sheriff; I was telling your beauteous bride the story of yon church bells.

Sheriff. That will do for some other chime!

Annabel. Oh a passing, pleasant story, methinks. (*Aside to Allan.*) What was it?

Allan. Of a damsel who was charmed away from a hapless marriage by hearing those bells ring out their chimes.

THE BELLS OF ST. SWITHINS.

Allan.   In olden times
                     St. Swithins' chimes

Told blithely ev'ry hour
From out the old grey tower.
'Neath Swithins' shade
A lovely maid
Lived in a cottage bower,
As fair as any flower.
She heard the chimes through all the day ;
She heard them call the folk to pray ;
She learned to love their roundelay
From old St. Swithins' tower.

Ding, dong, bell,
For wedding song or funeral knell,
Your message to each hearer tell,
Betimes,
Ye chimes.
Ding, dong, dong !
Of joy or grief may be your song.
If mirth or pain
Be your refrain,
Still ring, ye bells, and sing.

All. Ding, dong, bell—etc.

Allan. A youth there came
With love aflame
To that sweet maiden's bower
Beneath St. Swithins' tower.
With smile and sigh
He bade her fly
Nor heed what clouds might lower—
True love enough for dower—
A little space with him she strayed,
When warningly those chime bells played :
" Turn back, turn back, O gentle maid,
His love will last an hour."

All. Ding, dong, bell—etc.

(After the song, all exit. Robin Hood enters, still wearing his monk's dress.)

Robin. It is all prepared. The chapel will be filled with our brave fellows. I will be in the Bishop's place, with Little John and Scarlet at either hand. It will be strange indeed if we cannot carry off both girls and baffle the Sheriff.

(Friar Tuck appears in the window of the jail.)

Friar T. What, ho ! Captain Robin Hood ! How much longer must I cool my heels in this box ? These chains are a misfit. And I'm getting hungry. Can't you get one a tripe sandwich ?

Robin. Patience, my jovial Friar, you will soon be released. You must rattle your chains loudly. Then if the Sheriff hears them he will not imagine that I have escaped. (*Friar Tuck rattles chains loudly.*)

Friar T. But begone. I see some one approaching from the Sheriff's house.

Robin. Perhaps it may be Marian. I will stay and tell her of our plan. (*Retires up stage. Marian enters from the house.*)

Marian. What! It is Robin!

Robin Yes, my Marian—mine in spite of the King's command.

Marian. But how have you managed to escape?

Robin. That I have not time to tell you now. I come to tell you that you must keep up a good heart, and at the very moment that this Guy of Gisborne thinks to make you his wife I will save you.

Marian. The king has returned from the Crusades. If you can contrive to gain a little time, His Majesty is sure to right your wrongs and to give me to you instead of to that impostor, Guy of Gisborne.

Robin. Yes, I have sent one of my trusty comrades with a message to His Majesty. If I know that you still love me, you may trust to me and the valor of Robin Hood's band.

Marian. My brave Robin. Come what may, I will be yours and yours only.

(*Robin exits. Marian remains. Sheriff enters.*)

Sheriff. What's this? Another monk monking? Marian talking to a strange man on her wedding day. Your betrothed, the Earl, will positively sizzle with jealousy.

Marian. It was only the Friar, who has been giving me wise counsel to be obedient and dutiful.

Sheriff And now to give Robin his invitation to your wedding.

Marian. What? Is he to be among the guests?

Sheriff. Certainly. It will add to my triumph if he stands by in his chains and sees you wedded to his rival. (*Opens the door of the jail.*) Ho, master outlaw, come forth. (*Leaves the door open. Turns to talk to Marian.*) Now you shall see what a shamefaced fellow this Robin is. This is my moment for gloating. You may want to gloat sometime yourself, so just watch me and you will pick up a few points. Come forth, my bold outlaw. Now you shall see what a shamefaced fellow this Robin is. Come forth!

(*Friar Tuck enters.*)

Sheriff. So, so; you claim to be the rightful Earl of Huntington, do you? (*Sees that it is not Robin.*) What's this? Robin seems to have shrunk and grown fat. Little Robin Red vest. What means this trick, sirrah? Robin Hood escaped! Ho, to the gallows with this fellow!

Friar T. Gallows? Thou impious rascal! I am a churchman, a friar. Around my form I draw the magic circle. Step but one foot within it, and I will curse you up hill and down dale. A gallows for a friar, for-sooth. Try it !

Sheriff. But where is Robin ?

Friar T. Oh, you mean the wight who robbed me of my cowl and gown and put his chains on me. I went to his cell to give him kindly coun-sel, when he overpowered me and escaped. Out upon him, say I !

Marian. Since Robin has escaped. I suppose you will postpone the wed-dings ?

Sheriff. Postpone the weddings? Nonsense ! Go and prepare yourself at once. Then we will summon the King's archers and scour the coun-try for Robin Hood. Go, girl, and prepare.

Marian. I must trust to Robin to find some means to defeat the Sheriff's plans. (*She enters the house. Guy enters. Dame Durden comes on, dragging Annabel.*)

Dame. Come along, you foolish girl. Would you believe it, Master Sheriff, this child is not eager to marry you?

Sheriff. Well, there's no accounting for tastes.

Guy. Strange to say, Marian is not yearning to marry me.

Friar T. Sensible girls, both of them.

Annabel. (*To Sheriff.*) You old villain, trying to steal a girl from her sweetheart. Oh, I'll get even with you, if I have to marry you to do it. I'll make it warm for you.

Sheriff. My dear, I expect that. When a man gets married, he must take his chances. But I am of a cheerful disposition. Make it warm for me, if you can ; but the more you scold, the more I will sing. I have never seen the trials that I could not chase away by singing my tooral-looral lay.

QUINTETTE. *Annabel, Dame Durden, Sheriff, Friar and Guy.*

I.

When life seems made of pains and pangs,
I sing my tooral-looral lay.
When bill collectors spout harangues.
I sing my tooral-looral lay.
No matter what care
On us may bear,
What though our clothes be out of style,
Though poverty's ills
Bring bitter pills,
We'll swallow them and smile
The while,
While songs our woes beguile.
As life is brief, let life be gay,
It only lasts a summer day ;

So carking care pray chase away
By singing tiddy-fal-lay.

II.

When no one laughs at jokes I make,
I sing my tooral-looral lay ;
And when I have a hard toothache,
I sing my tooral-looral lay ;
When dinners are cold
And old wives scold,
I sing until my throat is sore ;
When terrible gout
Doth make me shout,
I only sing the more,
Yes, more,
Than e'er I sang before.
As life is short, let life be gay, etc.

Sheriff. Come. To the church. As the Bishop of Hereford has been captured by that villain, Robin Hood, this worthy Friar will perform the ceremony.

Robin. Yes, my Lord Sheriff, I am very much at your service.

Guy. Come, let the wedding proceed at once.

Sheriff. Yes, to the church.

All. To the church.

FINALE.

Sheriff. Now let each bonny bridegroom take his bride ;
The doors of yonder church, pray open wide.

Friar T. To open those church doors there is no need ;
For in that task will others take the lead.

Allan. (Aside.) You shall not wed these damsels ; no ;
Your plans we yet will overthrow.

Annabel. (Aside.) I will obey that fateful chime,
If Robin should not come in time.

(*The doors of the church are thrown open. Robin stands in front of the doors, throws his friar's gown aside and shows himself in a suit of green. The church is filled with armed outlaws clad in Lincoln green.*)

Outlaws. Vict'ry ! We conquer at last.

Marian. Danger is over and past.

Robin. Love, now we never more will part,
Whate'er betide.
Safe in my sheltering arms thou art,
My own sweet bride.

Sheriff.	With rage I burn.
Outlaws.	We win the day.
	Now away
	To Sherwood Forest without delay.

(Trumpets sound without.)

All.   What is this ?

(A messenger enters with a letter.)

Little J.   A pardon from the King for Robin Hood.
Robin.   My pardon !
Marian.   Then he is free
                  To wed with me.

Robin.   You see, Master Sheriff, at last I play the King.
Sheriff.   Oh, promise me that some day you will die.
Marian.   I came as a cavalier ;
        'Twas to seek my own and only love.
           Tho' clouds were dark and drear,
        Yet the sky is now blue above.

Robin.   Farewell to old Sherwood gay,
        And to all my gallant outlaw crew ;
          But many a match we yet may have
        With my true bow of yew.

All.   Danger's past, and at last
        They'll be married ; their love's steadfast.
        May they ne'er know a care,
        May their lives be always fair.
        May they never have to sever,
          Hail the happy pair.

END OF THE OPERA.

NEW NATIONAL THEATRE

W. H. RAPLEY - - - - - - - - MANAGER
T. ARTHUR SMITH - - - - - - - - Treasurer

WEEK OF MONDAY, OCTOBER 31, 1898.

SATURDAY MATINEE

THE BOSTONIANS

BARNABEE & MACDONALD, Proprietors.

Direction FRANK L. PERLEY.

IN THEIR MOST POPULAR OPERA,

Robin Hood.

By REGINALD DEKOVEN AND HARRY B. SMITH.

CAST OF CHARACTERS.

Sheriff of Nottingham - - -	Henry Clay Barnabee
Little John - - - - - -	W. H. MacDonald
Robin Hood - - - - -	William E. Philp
Will Scarlet - - - - -	William McDonald
Alan a-Dale - - - - -	Jessie Bartlett Davis
Friar Tuck - - - - -	George Frothingham
Guy of Gisborne - - - - -	W. H. Fitzgerald
Maid Marion - - - - -	Helen Bertram
Dame Durden - - - -	Josephine Bartlett
Annabel - - - - -	Carolyn Daniels

SYNOPSIS OF SCENES.

ACT I.—Market Square, Nottingham, England.
ACT II.—Sherwood Forest, England.
ACT III.—Courtyard of the Sheriff's House.

Friday Afternoon, November 4th, at 4 o'clock. and Sunday Evening,
November 6th, at 8.15 o'clock,

Mr. HALL CAINE

Will deliver his unique lecture HOME SWEET HOME.

NEXT
WEEK } **Charles Frohman's Comedians**
PRESENTING
WILLIAM GILLETTE'S Latest Comedy Hit,
BECAUSE SHE LOVED HIM SO.

Sunday Evening December 11th,

Col. R. C. Ingersoll will deliver his Superstition